D0508755

PONY CAMP diaries

Megan and Mischief

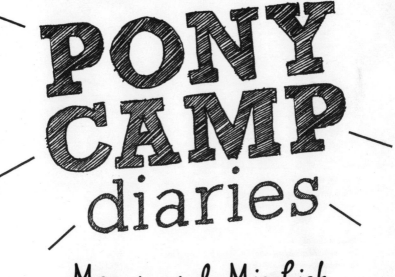

STRIPES PUBLISHING
An imprint of the Little Tiger Group
1 Coda Studios, 189 Munster Road,
London SW6 6AW

A paperback original
First published in Great Britain by Stripes Publishing in 2007
This edition published in 2018

Text copyright © Kelly McKain 2007, 2018
Illustration © Mandy Stanley 2007, 2018

ISBN: 978-1-84715-978-6

A CIP catalogue record for this book is available from the British Library.

Printed and bound in the UK.

10 9 8 7 6 5 4 3 2 1

PONY CAMP
diaries

Megan and Mischief

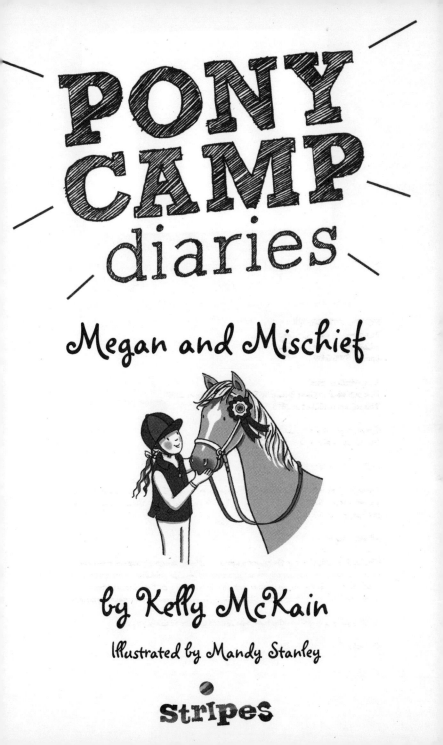

by Kelly McKain

Illustrated by Mandy Stanley

stripes

For Millie (star rider!), Jody (star mum!)
and the whole Wallington crew.

With thanks to Jodie Maile (star instructor!) for getting
me back in the saddle and for her invaluable help
and advice with this book.

And special thanks to Rose, Prince
and Janet Rising (star consultant!)

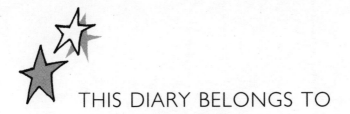

THIS DIARY BELONGS TO

MEGAN
☆ THE ☆
BRAVE!

Dear Riders,

A warm welcome to Sunnyside Stables!

Sunnyside is our home and for the next week it will be yours too! We're a big family – my husband Johnny and I have two children, Millie and James, plus two dogs ... and all the ponies, of course!

We have friendly yard staff and a very talented instructor, Sally, to help you get the most out of your week. If you have any worries or questions about anything at all, just ask. We're here to help, and we want your holiday to be as enjoyable as possible – so don't be shy!

As you know, you will have a pony to look after as your own for the week. Your pony can't wait to meet you and start having fun! During your stay, you'll be caring for your pony, improving your riding, enjoying long country hacks, learning new skills and making friends.

And this week's special activity is a breathtaking beach ride. Just imagine you and your pony cantering across the sand together! Add swimming, games, films, barbecues and a gymkhana and you're in for a fun-filled holiday to remember!

This special Pony Camp Diary is for you to fill with all your holiday memories. We hope you'll write all about your adventures here at Sunnyside Stables – because we know you're going to have lots!

Wishing you a wonderful time with us!

Jody xx

menage
men
stables x4
farmhouse
&
garden
stables x2
yard
pool
Tack
room
Car park
office
Ponty
lower field

Monday 9.16 am

Wow! I'm actually here at Pony Camp! At last!
Jody, who runs Sunnyside Stables, gave me this
fabulous Pony Camp diary to write down my
adventures this week. There's even a space on
the cover to stick a picture of MY pony – I
can't wait to meet him … or her! I wonder
who I'll get?! Typically, Mum and Dad got me
here mega early and no one else has come
yet, so I'm starting right this second! Jody gave
me a map, too, and a timetable, and we're
having a gymkhana on Friday with prizes
and everything – SO exciting!! I've
never entered any competitions before
and I'd love to win a rosette for my pony
pinboard at home. That would be brilliant!

When Mum and Dad were registering me in
the office, which is in the yard, I had a sneaky
peek around and this place is amazing!

I saw a really huge horse in the stables, the kind that pulls ploughs. I hope I don't get him 'cos he's massive!

There were these two cute cheeky ponies tied up in the yard too, getting their tails washed by a girl with curly blonde hair, but they'd be too small for me. Then I noticed a huge field up the track that had lots more ponies in, including a cute cobby piebald and a prancing palomino. I can't wait to find out which one will be mine!

I'm so nervous it feels as if my Rice Krispies are doing a dance in my stomach!

I've never stayed away from home on my own before and I'm extra specially jittery 'cos of this secret thing I did. On the booking form, in the comments section, I put that I would like a forward-going pony!

♡ Megan and Mischief ♡

This is a big wow because at my riding
school I always end up with the slow ones. I'm
too shy to say anything though, so people think
I like lumbering along at the back of the ride
having to use my legs like crazy just to get a tiny
trot. But I'm ready for a challenge now – and
Pony Camp is it! No one knows me here so
I'm going to be a different girl. Not Megan who
still has a nightlight on in the hall and won't
join in with football in the park in case she gets
whacked in the head by accident. But a whole
new kind of Megan…

I'm even hoping to do some more jumping
while I'm here (I've only had a couple of tries
so far).

I'm lying on my bunk bed writing this. I've
bagsied the bottom one which is cool 'cos you
can hang your towel down from the bed above
and it makes a secret camp. I've already hidden
my tuckbox under my bed in case we get to
have a midnight feast! I can't wait to meet the
girls I'm sharing with. And most of all I can't
wait to see which pony I'm getting!

Oh, gotta go, some of the other girls are
here now… (I really hope they like me!)

P.S. I just met my room-mates, Millie and
Gabrielle. Millie is Jody's daughter and she lives
here all the time (how lucky is that?!) and she's
got her own pony, called Tally (how even
luckier is that?!). Gabrielle is really nice too
(phew!). She has these cool pony hair bobbles,
and me and Millie just helped her plait her long
wavy blonde hair and it looks really cool. I'm
going to buy the exact same ones
the second I get home.

Gabrielle's
hair
bobbles

14

Still Monday,
after yummy lunch

I GOT MY PONY!!

He's called Mischief and he's completely
gorgeous. Here's a quick profile of him:

U Megan's Pony Profile

star

socks

NAME: Mischief

HEIGHT: 13 hh

AGE: 6

BREED: Arab cross

COLOUR: Palomino

MARKINGS: Star and stripe, and white socks on hind legs

FAVE FOODS: Pony nuts and carrots

PERSONALITY: Really sweet but a bit cheeky (I'll write
   more about that later!)

15

Before we got our ponies, Jody did a welcome
talk and introduced us to all the staff. Lydia is
the girl with blonde curly hair who I saw before.
She's a stable hand, which is my dream job –
imagine getting paid to look after ponies all day!
Sally is the instructor and she has these cool
army print half chaps that I've wanted since I
saw them in *Pony* magazine. Jody looks after
us and does all the cooking (we're all going to
help too, but she's in charge) and her husband
Johnny is the Yard Manager and Millie's dad!

Next Jody got us to say our names and
where we were from. There are nine of us
including Millie, three in each room. Carla is

the youngest (she's only six) and she's in with Chloe and Tam, these two friends who came all the way from Manchester! In the other room there are three almost-teenagers sharing together – Kate and Karen the twins are smiley and nice, but Jade looks a bit moody. She wears lots of make-up and has blonde hair that she keeps flicking round as if she's in a shampoo ad.

Anyway, back to MY PONY!

When Lydia led this gorgeous pony out of the stable I crossed my fingers really tight, hoping he was for me. Then I heard Sally say, "Megan, you asked for a challenge, so we'll try you on Mischief."

I could hardly believe it! He was the gorgeous palomino I'd seen in the field! I wanted to jump up and down and scream, "Yes! Yes! Yes!" but I didn't in case it spooked the ponies.

Kate got this handsome black gelding called Rupert.

Gabrielle

got the cute cobby piebald, who's called Prince.

Moody Jade

got a glossy chestnut called Shine, who flicks her tail round in the same way Jade does with her hair –

so they suit each other well! I don't remember who the others got because I was too excited about Mischief!

We tacked up (Lydia helped me with getting the bit in) and waited to mount up on the block, ready for our first lesson. Once I was on I felt quite high up on Mischief, but as he's

a light build I could wrap my legs round his sides nicely. I even tightened my own girth, and I felt really cool and grown up just sorting it out myself – until Mischief started wandering off while I still had my leg forward. Lydia had to come back over and hold him still, so then I didn't feel very cool after all!

At first, when we got in the manège we just had to walk round on the track and think about sitting up straight and keeping our hands relaxed and our heels down. There were no complete beginners and everyone could trot at least, so that was okay.

Then it all went not okay, 'cos Mischief started doing Cheeky Things. Like:

Cheeky Thing 1

We did trotting to the back of the ride one by one and I think Mischief got bored of walking round and round waiting for his turn because

he kept going really close to the person in front, which was Gabby, and nearly sticking his nose up Prince's tail. Sally told me to use half halts to keep him in check, but that didn't really work because he just kept stopping completely!

Cheeky Thing 2

When it was our turn and I asked for trot, Mischief just leaped backwards and started skittering about. Everyone was looking at me and I felt really panicky, but then Sally strode towards us and so Mischief started behaving after all. Well, until…

Cheeky Thing 3

When we did some practice of going over trotting poles, Mischief got a bit excited and barged up the side of Shine. I pulled on the reins and leaned back but I still crashed legs with Moody Jade. I'm sure it didn't hurt but she

made a big fuss, crying, "Argh!" really loudly and saying that I'd got no control. I pretended not to hear, but I just KNOW everyone else was listening. After that I tried really hard to keep out of trouble but...

Cheeky Thing 4

We were going round cones and  Mischief went absolutely miles round them, like way over to the edge of the manège. Sally called out, "Time to take charge and get tough, Megan!" which was awful because it was like being told off in front of everyone and I was already trying my hardest – but Mischief was just ignoring me!

But the worst thing was when Sally asked some of us to ride our ponies into the middle (including me!) while the others had a canter

21

round the track. I was really upset because I've done loads of cantering on Fella back at home, even if it was only short bursts after lots of encouraging him.

I'm worried that Sally thinks I'm not a very good rider. I really want to win something in the gymkhana and have another try at jumping. But for that to happen I'll have to get tough with Mischief like she said. But HELP! How do I do that? I'm not the sort of person who usually gets tough about anything. Usually I tell Dad and he gets tough for me, like when Julian Mason put a snowball down my back at school and Dad rang up Mr Thomas the head. But Dad isn't here to help me now! I'll just have to turn into Megan the Brave and show Mischief who's

Oh, time to go again!

Still Monday (just!)

Millie lent me her torch so I'm writing this in bed after lights out!

I'm totally whacked — we've done so much already and it's only the first day.

After our lessons we had a lecture on grooming and I found out what the different curry combs are for. (I'm not one of the girls who helps out on the yard where I ride at home, so I don't know much about grooming.) Then we

Currycomb

had tea and a swim in the pool for our Evening Activity. Me and Millie and Gabrielle were doing synchronized swimming — well, trying to anyway, and we ended up in total hysterics. I'm so lucky to have such great room-mates! And Millie is so lucky to live here all the time!

Gabrielle is in the bunk above me, so I'm scribbling this really quietly 'cos she's fast asleep.

She has an iPod and before tea she let me listen on one of the earphones, even though they're the little ones you stick right in your ears and she could have thought yuck and not wanted me to share it!

Well, Mischief did three more Cheeky Things this afternoon, including nearly making me fall off when we were riding without stirrups by skittering about when Lydia pushed a wheelbarrow past. I tried really hard to be Megan the Brave but I felt like crying when we dismounted. Gabrielle gave me a hug and Millie said, "Don't worry, it can be hard getting used to a new pony and Mischief isn't called Mischief for nothing!"

Best friends!

♘ Megan and Mischief ♘

I said, "But everyone thinks I'm rubbish!" and Millie said, "No one thinks that." But I think she was just being nice 'cos we both heard Jade giggling when I lost my balance. At that moment I suddenly missed Mum and Dad so much.

Sally called me over when we were untacking and asked if I wanted to swap on to this other pony called Star who is very reliable. I know reliable means slow, as in another plodder. I could feel myself almost starting to cry but I managed to hold it in and say I wanted to stick with Mischief.

STAR - reliable but probably another plodder!!

Sally said, "Okay, that's fine for now, but I'll just have to keep an eye on how things go. I want you to get the most out of your week here, Megan, and I'm sure you do too."

Phew! But I can't believe she asked me to swap. I will have to get tougher if I want to keep my gorgeous Mischief – and quickly!

After the Grooming Lecture we did the Practical Learning which meant fully grooming our ponies from head to hoof. Lydia came round to give us help, and I got to try out the plastic curry comb to lift the mud and grease out of Mischief's coat. When I was brushing round his shoulder with the dandy brush he nuzzled up to me, so I think he loves me too!

I even secretly pretended that he was my very own pony and that we'd come here for a holiday together, with him in a horsebox.

I can't wait for tomorrow because we get to go on the yard straight after breakfast and do

jobs like real pony-owners! I'm going up to the field with the other girls whose ponies live out, to catch them and bring them down to the yard.

I didn't ring Mum and Dad tonight even though we had the choice after tea because I was still a bit upset about my bad lesson and I didn't want Mum to worry (which she does quite a lot). I'll make a new start tomorrow and prove to everyone that I can handle Mischief and then I'll have something great to tell them both on the phone!

Night night,
sleep tight!
Sweet pony dreams
'til morning light!

Tuesday 11.06 am,
before the beach ride

Oh! I fell asleep last night after writing my diary so we didn't get to have a midnight feast. Hopefully we will tonight!

Right now it's morning break and everyone's getting ready to go on the beach ride, so I'm quickly writing this. I have had such a fab time this morning with my lovely Mischief!

This is what we did:

8.20 am
Brought in the ponies. We also did a quick bit of grooming and picked out their feet. Mischief had a big stone quite near his frog so I had to be very gentle and careful.

9.00 am, breakfast time

This was cool because there are lots of little
boxes of cereals to choose from and you can
have any kind you want, or even mix two sorts
together. I had Ricicles and Coco Pops, which
I'm not normally allowed because of all the
sugar.

9.30 am

Normally we would get our ponies ready for
the first lesson but it's different today because
we're going on the beach ride! So instead
we had our lecture, which was on how to
do bandaging and put on boots. This is really
important for travelling because if you bandage
up your pony's tail it won't rub while he's in the
horsebox. And putting on boots or bandages
stops his legs getting knocked if there's a sudden
jolt or slamming of brakes!

First Lydia did a demonstration on her bay,

29

Shy, and then we all had a go on our ponies.
We're only taking four ponies to the beach
(Tally, Rupert, Twinkle and Mischief – yippee!)
but we practised on our own ponies anyway.
Lydia showed us how to tie them up on the
yard safely and then how to put a bale of straw
between you and your pony's hind legs just in
case they spook and kick backwards (not that
Mischief would ever kick me because he is
my gorgeous wonderhorse!). My tail bandage
went a bit wrong at first and it
all unravelled halfway and hung
down like streamers. But Lydia
showed me that I could start it off
quite tight around the dock without

I did it
wrong!

hurting Mischief and then
it held together better (although it
still wasn't perfect).

Still not
perfect!

Then we got to lead the beach-ride ponies up the track to the horseboxes. On the way I secretly pretended that Mischief was my own pony again and that we were going back to the horsebox to go home together. I got so excited watching Johnny and Lydia load them up. I've never ridden on the beach before and Millie says it's really fun. I've got to go now because she's saving the back seat of her dad's Land Rover for me and her and Gabrielle, even though everyone else has to go in the minibus!

Two minutes later!

Oh dear, my happy mood is ruined!

I'm writing this in the back of the Land Rover as we're still waiting for everyone else to pile into the minibus. As I was walking over to the Land Rover, I spotted Moody Jade having a strop because Shine isn't going to the beach and she has to ride Rupert after Kate instead. I wanted to try and make friends with her after the leg-crashing thing, so I tried to be nice by saying, "Don't worry, Jade, it's only for one ride." But she just sneered at me and said, "What do you know? Your pony's coming with us, which is so not fair, 'specially when you can't even handle him properly!"

I just stood there staring at her with my legs shaking and my eyes filling up with tears. And then she did this really mean "What are you staring at?" look.

Millie just this minute read this and said, "Don't let her spoil your trip," and she's right. In fact, I'm just going to keep out of her way from now on.

Before tea,
back from the beach!

WOW! The beach ride was amazing! I was in the first group with Millie and Chloe. Kate was meant to be riding with us too, as Rupert is her pony, but Jade made such a fuss Kate let her go first (boo!).

We were on a private beach that the owners let Sunnyside use, so there were no people around. While we tacked up, Sally warned Jade not to ride too close to the sea as Rupert doesn't like the water. Jade just harrumphed and said, "Well then, why couldn't we bring Shine instead?" Sally just smiled and said, "Come on, cheer up and try to enjoy yourself," which just made Jade look even more grumpy.

34

As soon as we mounted I felt really nervous
about being out of the school because I've
never even been on a hack out before. I kept
thinking that Mischief might just suddenly take
off down the beach, but Lydia spotted me
looking scared and came and held on to him. I
wasn't embarrassed at all – just glad!

Then we were off! Sally rode at the back on
her own horse, Blue, and Millie was at the front
on Tally. Lydia rode Shy along beside us – she
had a lead rope clipped to her D ring, which
made me feel really safe. We walked on for a
while, getting used to the sand, which felt softer
than the woodchips in the manège. Then we
moved into a trot. It was so brilliant jogging
along in sitting trot and when we went rising I
wasn't thinking "up, down, up, down" like usual
but just sort of doing it. Mischief had lots of
impulsion and I only had to lightly squeeze my
lower leg against him, so it was far easier than

normal for me to keep it all together and not flap about. And it wasn't scary at all – it was fab! I wasn't worried about hitting the fences at the sides like I am in the manège. And we didn't have to do any turns or try to stay on a track, we just had to go straight forward, so I felt much more like Megan the Brave than Megan the Terrified. Millie was right about beach rides. It was brilliant!

ME TODAY!
Megan the BRAVE!

Sally said my new confidence showed in my seat and hands, and that's why Mischief was listening to me, and I couldn't help smiling. We went back to walk then and Sally corrected our positions and ran through the aids for going into canter, just as a reminder. We picked up rising trot again and when she gave the word we went sitting and asked for canter. Millie and Tally were off like a rocket, then Rupert and Jade, and then me and Mischief! I tried to sit still and not throw my body forward, which is my number one bad habit, and for once I just kept my seat and went with the rhythm and it felt like we were flying!

I don't know if I should write about what happened next, in case Jade somehow finds out and starts not liking me even more, but this is my diary and I want to put what truly happened so here goes. As we cantered up the beach, Jade kept nudging Rupert over into the waves

and so Sally called, "Jade, stay on the sand, please. I've already told you Rupert doesn't like the water."

But Jade didn't listen and just rode closer and closer to the sea. Just as Sally said crossly, "Right, and easing back into trot everyone," this wave broke on Rupert and he sort of leaped backwards and Jade lost her stirrup.

Then just as she was trying to get it back, Rupert went back into trot really suddenly and she bobbled forwards, clinging to his neck. She probably could have sat up, except then he dropped his head and snorted loudly and she toppled off into the sea! It was so funny because it looked like Rupert had dumped her there on purpose.

(Maybe he had!)

Me and Millie couldn't help laughing!

But Jade herself was NOT finding it funny! Instead she was rolling about clutching her leg and groaning. As Sally dismounted and checked her over, I stopped laughing and started to worry that she'd seriously hurt herself. But Sally said, "You're fine, just a bit wet, that's all. I did warn you not to go near the water."

"I didn't!" grumped Jade. "It was Rupert's fault!" But Sally just raised one eyebrow and said, "Let's not argue about it. You're okay and that's the main thing."

Sally gave Jade a leg up but she was still grumbling about the fall. I forgot not to look at her so she did the "What are you staring at?" face to me again, and I quickly turned away and started talking to Millie. But it really made my stomach churn because I can't stand it if someone doesn't like me. We just walked and trotted on the way back, and even though Jade

was still grumbling, she rode on the exact bit of sand that Sally told her to and not a single millimetre closer to the water.

When we got back to the picnic place everyone wanted to know why Jade was dripping wet. She was really snappy and wouldn't tell them, so while Jody helped her to dry off, Millie explained about the fall. Everyone laughed and Moody Jade got even moodier.

I didn't join in the laughing, hoping she'd notice, but she just flounced off round the back of the horsebox to change into the dry stuff Jody had brought "just in case".

Then the second group got ready to ride.
I held on to Mischief while Gabrielle mounted
and I kept giving her all these tips about being
confident and relaxed with him and sitting up
tall but she just smiled and said, "Megan, chill, I'll
be fine!"

Kate was on Rupert and when Sally warned
her about the water thing she laughed and
said, "Don't worry, there's no way I'm going
near the sea, not after what happened to Jade!"
That made everyone start laughing again, which
made Moody Jade even crosser.

I watched Gabrielle heading off on Mischief
and I only felt a tiny bit jealous! Then we had
our picnic lunch, with cheese and tomato or
tuna and cucumber sandwiches. I had one of
each without picking out the cucumber or
the tomato. Eating what I'm given is part of
me being Megan the Brave, instead of
Megan the Fussy like I am at home.

41

After that, Chloe got her model horses out, which are the cool Breyer ones, and we all played with them (except Moody Jade, who read a Popworld mag and ignored us). We made up a whole game about running the only riding school in the Sahara desert, and we even shaped some of the sand and pebbles into a jumping course! I chose the palomino, of course, and pretended that it was Mischief and that I was riding him over these really high jumps and winning heaps of rosettes.

On the way home in the Land Rover, Gabrielle told me that she'd had fun on Mischief, but she wished Prince had gone on the trip instead and she said she couldn't wait to get back and see him. I was secretly glad because I don't want anyone else to start loving Mischief when he's MINE!

I ♡ Mischief

In bed, in the dark with Millie's torch!

I'm waiting for midnight so we can have our secret feast! We all made a pact to stay up till exactly twelve o'clock, but it's only ten past ten and Millie and Gabrielle are both fast asleep. Still, I don't mind waiting by myself because I've got lots to write. At midnight I'm going to wake them up so we can have the rest of my sweets and the strawberry laces that Gabrielle brought and talk about ponies and maybe even tell ghost stories. Millie says she knows a great one about a headless horseman (eek!).

Well, I did phone Mum and Dad tonight, and I told them all about how well the beach ride had gone and how pleased Sally was with my riding. Mum got a bit worried about us cantering on the beach and I had to convince her that it was all perfectly safe and that I had my body protector on and my chin strap done up and long sleeves and my proper boots and everything.

My stomach churned up a bit when I put the phone down, like it did when Jade pulled her "What are you staring at?" face at me on the beach. I've hardly thought about Mum and Dad since I've been here but speaking to them made me miss them so much.

I cheered up during the Evening Activity though, which was a table tennis tournament. Millie was ace and me and Gabrielle were rubbish, but it didn't matter because it was so much fun!

Millie's dad pretended to be joining in just because he was the grown-up who had to organize us, but we could tell he had practised loads and was really trying to win. Karen beat him in the final though, and we all cheered, and she won a cool pony pencil case with all new things in it.

It's only the second day of Pony Camp and I've already learned about bandaging and grooming and been cantering on the beach, and made some completely fab friends and met Mischief, my star pony – this really is a dream holiday!

Oh, I just had a big yawn. Maybe I'll close my eyes for a minute or two.

Wednesday morning

I can't believe we all slept straight through
midnight — again! Today is really exciting because
we're learning the games we'll be playing in the
gymkhana on Friday. Well, some people know
them already so it's just practice for them, but
I don't! There was this one gymkhana at our
stable that I was going to be in, but at the last
minute I got scared and wimped out and just
ended up watching with Mum. But this time I
am going to do it!

I'm really looking forward to riding Mischief
after we did so well yesterday on the beach.
He came straight up to the gate this morning
and let me put on his headcollar and lead rope
without any problems at all. I'm sure everything
will go brilliantly from now on and Sally will see
that I'm a good rider and Jade will be AMAZED
and start liking me.

After the lesson

Oh dear. I've had the worst morning ever.
I'm trying really hard not to cry but my writing
hand is shaking loads. The others are having
their break downstairs but I didn't feel like eating
anything so I'm lying on my bed writing this.

Things started off okay-ish with the relay
race. I'm really getting a better position in
canter now, although I still couldn't turn
smoothly at the top so I lost lots of ground for
the way back. But when we were doing the
egg and spoon race I had to put both reins in
one hand and Mischief suddenly swerved off his
track and ran across the other ponies' lanes for
no reason. Jade got cross with me because she
had to slow Shine down to keep from crashing
into us. When I finally managed to halt
she shouted, "If you can't control that
pony you shouldn't be on it!"

47

Even though she made me feel really shaky I knew I had to defend Mischief. "Mischief is not an 'it', he's a 'he'," I said, trying not to let my voice wobble. "And anyway, ponies are unpredictable. You can't always tell what they'll do."

Jade made that harrumphing sound she always does and said, "Don't blame that nag for your mistakes!" Then she turned Shine and trotted back to the start line, her egg perfectly balanced on her spoon.

Huh! How dare she call Mischief a nag! I rode back to the start line too, still grumbling, and Millie said, "Don't worry about her, she's just really moody. It's nothing personal."

But I think it IS personal. Jade doesn't seem to pick on anyone else. Why is it always me? I was upset about Jade for the rest of the lesson, so I wasn't very brave for the other races, like the apple bobbing and the bending. And when

we practised the Chase Me Charlie I was only half concentrating because of trying to avoid Jade's eye, so I got knocked out on the first hole. Also, in a lot of the races we had to turn when we reached the far end of the manège and then canter back, and I just couldn't get it right. Mischief kept going along on the track, like in a normal lesson, and the harder I tried to pull him round the more wrong it seemed to go. Sally kept telling me to relax my hands and use more leg, but I just couldn't get it together. So then she told me to put the reins in one hand and hold on to the pommel if I felt unsteady. That's what you do when you're just beginning!

I really want Mum and Dad to be proud of me on Friday at the gymkhana but at this rate I'm never going to win anything!

After we'd dismounted, Sally called me over
for a "chat". Except it wasn't really a chat 'cos
I let her do all the talking. I knew if I opened
my mouth to say anything I'd start crying.
Sally explained that she might have to swap
me off Mischief for the rest of the week. She
said, "Megan, it's very difficult for you to enjoy
yourself or learn new skills when you're having
such basic problems with control."

She doesn't understand that it's not just
about the riding, Mischief is my pony and I
love him so much I couldn't stand for us to be
apart. And I am enjoying myself, mostly. All the
grooming and tacking up is so much fun and the
beach ride was brilliant. But when I opened my
mouth to say that to Sally, nothing came out
except "But I love him!" in a teary, croaky voice.

Sally said, more softly, "I'll have to talk to
Johnny and Jody about it, and I'll let you know
after lunch, okay?"

All I could do was nod, but inside my
thoughts were racing. What will the others think
if I get swapped off Mischief? What will Jade say?
Will Mischief think I don't love him any more?

Oh, Millie's calling up the stairs for me. At
least we have our Stable Management lecture
next, about feeds and pony health, so I can
do my Practical Learning with Mischief. He's
definitely mine till after lunch and I want to
spend every second I can with him, before the
worst might happen.

Afternoon - in our bedroom
(the others aren't back yet)

I'm writing this while I'm waiting for the others
to come back from their afternoon ride out.
I didn't go, which is a long story but I'll try
to write it all down in here before Millie and
Gabrielle get back.

Well, I felt really ill after lunch with a tummy
ache – it must have been the fish fingers.
Gabrielle and Millie tried to take my mind off it,
but then it got worse so Jody suggested I have
a lie down. I went and cuddled up on my bed
with Millie's black Labrador, Ponty, and tried not
to think about Sally's decision.

Millie came to get me just before the hack,
but I still didn't feel well, so
she went down and told
Sally and Sally said
I could miss it.

52

○ Megan and Mischief ○

When everyone had gone, Jody came in and sat down on the bed and asked if I was feeling any better. I started off talking about my stomach ache and ended up telling her about the disaster-filled gymkhana practice and how Sally might swap me off Mischief.

Jody smiled in a kind way. "Sally told me," she said. "And I wonder if you're not feeling well because you're worried about her decision."

I realized then that while it was mainly the fish fingers it might have been the worry as well, just a little bit. I nodded, and then I suddenly blurted out, "Sally thinks I'm rubbish."

Jody said, "Megan, that's nonsense. If you're not learning and improving then it's our fault for putting you on the wrong pony. We just want you to enjoy yourself."

"But I enjoy myself on Mischief!" I cried.

Jody gave me a look like she wasn't sure.

I said, "Well, maybe it's not exactly fun in the manège when he's playing up, but it was brill on the beach and I just love having him as my pony and grooming him and looking after him and..." I felt myself nearly start crying then. I really REALLY didn't want to lose Mischief. "It just feels as if he's mine," I sniffled.

Jody nodded. "Well, Megan, maybe we can do something about this. In the end it's Sally's decision, of course, but perhaps... Get your boots on and meet me in the yard by Mischief's stable in five minutes." Then she stood up and bustled out of the door.

By a lucky coincidence I didn't feel ill any more, so I went to the bathroom and washed my face, then went down to the porch, grabbed my crash hat and pulled on my boots. I poked my head round Mischief's stable door and there was Jody, tacking him up. She passed the girth to me and asked, "What's the thing you're

having the most difficulty with?"

"Everything," I grumbled, lifting the saddle flap and buckling it up.

"Well, let's just choose one thing to start with," she said, and even though I couldn't see her face, I could hear in her voice that she was smiling. "If Mischief knows you're going to keep trying till you get something right it'll make everything else easier too, because you'll have more confidence. And he'll know you mean business."

"Okay," I said, thinking quickly. "Can we work on turning a circle, because it was my worst thing this morning and so it's probably sticking in Sally's memory right now!"

Once we got into the manège, Mischief and I warmed up on both reins and rode a few circles in walk. Then we got to work and Jody explained that my outside leg controls the shape of the circle and my inside leg controls the size. She said I shouldn't think about turning more tightly, but more smoothly instead and she even gave me a schooling stick to gently tap Mischief with if he ignored my leg aids. Every time Mischief tried to fall in, Jody called, "Keep going, Megan! Leg! Leg! Leg!"

Well, I was giving it so much inside leg I thought my leg might actually fall off, but it still didn't work. I pulled hard on my outside rein to try and bring Mischief back on track, but all that happened was that his head twisted round and

his body stayed where it was.

"Relax!" called Jody. "You're so busy yanking those reins you've forgotten about your seat and legs. If you turn it into a battle of wills, I think we know who'll win!"

So I tried to relax my hands and concentrate on keeping a good leg and seat position.

It didn't work at first and Mischief still kept falling in and leaning on me, but I was determined not to give up. Jody called, "Sit up tall and look where you're meant to be going, rather than where you're afraid Mischief will actually go!" This made me laugh and then Jody laughed too and I started to feel a bit better. Jody was right – when I started acting like the boss, Mischief did stop being so cheeky.

Pretty soon I'd got the hang of riding a circle in trot from the A marker to the centre point and back round, without it looking triangle-shaped. I even managed to do some figure of eights to C!

"You see," said Jody. "You can do it!"

Then we practised cantering up to the end of the manège and the turn to come back again, like in the gymkhana games. Jody showed me how to make my turns tighter by using my body weight. At first it felt like just another complicated thing to remember, but then I started to get the idea. Jody was delighted and said we should stop there on a high note and that I'd done really well. By the end I felt brilliant, and I made a big fuss of Mischief too, to show him what a clever boy he is.

v. clever HORSE!

I could tell he was pleased with himself too, by the way he snorted and nuzzled up to me when I was leading him out of the manège.

Before today I couldn't understand it when Mischief ignored me, but now I know it's up to me to be clear in whatever I'm asking and not give up asking for it, and then everything works much better! With all Jody's help this afternoon I secretly think I might have a chance in the gymkhana, not to come first, but maybe to get a third or something.

Back on the yard, I got up the courage to ask Jody the BIG QUESTION, which was,

WILL I HAVE TO SWAP PONIES?

Jody sighed. "You know that's not up to me, Megan," she said. "But hopefully with what we've done today, you'll have improved enough to get more out of riding Mischief."

Yay! So she thinks we should stay together at least!

Jody let me tie Mischief up in the yard and groom him, with Lydia supervising me while she skipped out the surrounding stables and refilled the water buckets. When I was cleaning round Mischief's eyes with the pink sponge, I told him how well he'd done, and how much I love him. He sort of nodded his head down and blinked at me so I know for sure now that he loves me too. Then I had to explain the bad news that we might get separated. I could tell he was sad about that, so I gave him a big hug. But I also said that because of our good teamwork today we might be able to stay together, and he cheered up a tiny bit.

I can hear hooves in the yard – I'll go and help the others untack and turn out the ponies – and tell Millie and Gabrielle what happened this afternoon!

♘ Megan and Mischief ♘

It's Thursday, and I've just woken up (yawn)

Well, the rounders match last night was fun –
Tam turned out to be a great batter and Karen
scored loads for our team – but I was still
mainly thinking about Mischief and whether we
will be split up. We played in the field next door
to where the ponies live, so when I was fielding
I went really deep so I could watch Mischief
chomping the grass.

Me and Millie and Gabrielle didn't have a midnight feast last night — again! — even though I was actually still awake at exactly 12 o'clock. I decided not to wake them up because I was having a nice daydream (are they still called daydreams if you have them at night?) about Mischief and me rescuing a sheep that had fallen down a ditch.

I was also too busy being nervous about what Sally will decide. Now the moment is here and I've got to go down to the yard and find out the news…

♘ Megan and Mischief ♘

9.00 am, just before breakfast

Sally said I could stay on Mischief! Yes! Yes! Yes! And phew! Phew! Phew! 😊

The exact thing she said was, "Jody is also a qualified instructor and if she feels you've improved enough to keep riding Mischief, then that's fine by me, but you must keep up the good work and stay in control."

I said, "Yes, absolutely, I promise," and then I hurried straight over to Mischief's stable and told him the news. I gave him a big hug and I could tell he was as pleased as me by the way he nuzzled my neck. Yippee!

Mischief

Megan

It's especially brilliant because today we're all going on a picnic ride. We're having our lecture straight after breakfast and then getting our horses ready and we'll be out from about half eleven till half three in the afternoon, and we'll have our lunch out in the countryside too, which is the picnic bit! That is just so

COOL!

I can't wait!

And I'm going to show Moody Jade just what a fab team me and Mischief are too. Everything is brilliant again! Right, got to go and pick which cereals to mix up this morning.

Morning break

Oh dear, things have gone really wrong because I've fallen out with Millie and Gabrielle.

We were just having our orange and biscuits before we set off on the picnic ride and I was sitting next to Millie and kind of staring into space and thinking about whether Mum might get me the army print half chaps (I left *Pony* mag open on the kitchen table at the advert as a hint). Then Jade came up and said, "You look well edgy, Megan. I don't blame you. There's no way you'll be able to handle Mischief on the picnic ride."

"I'm not worried about anything," I said, determined not to get upset. "Am I, Millie?"

I expected Millie to say, "Course not," or something like that, but instead she just shrugged and looked at the table. "Well, I'm not," I mumbled. "Just because people are

staring into space thinking about half chaps, it doesn't mean they're worried."

Jade gave me a mean look and walked off, saying, "Well, you'd better not slow us up, that's all."

Right then, Gabrielle came over and asked Millie if she could ask Jody for more chocolate digestives because there were only custard creams left on the biscuit plate, and before I could stop myself I pointed at Millie and blurted out, "She thinks I'm not good enough to ride Mischief on the hack out!"

"I didn't say that!" Millie cried.

"But you didn't stick up for me when Jade said those things!" I challenged. I don't really know why I was so annoyed with her. I just was.

"Well, to be honest I am a bit worried about you," Millie admitted. "The picnic ride isn't the same as on the beach, Megan, where you can just point forward and poddle along."

"Huh! I do NOT poddle!" I cried.

"Okay, sorry, wrong word," said Millie, "but what I mean is, there are gates to open and you have to make sure Mischief doesn't barge through. And you need good control for the canters, otherwise you'll end up dragged through a hedge at the top of the field. And there might be cows that you have to stay calm round or you'll get Mischief all nervous and…"

Maybe what Millie was saying was sensible, but all I heard was, "You're not good enough to ride Mischief, and by the way you're not good enough to ride Mischief and, oh, did I mention that you're not good enough to ride Mischief?"

You're not good enough to ride Mischief!

"What do you think, Gabby?" I asked.

Gabrielle blushed bright red and looked at her feet. "Well, I guess you should listen to Millie," she mumbled. "I mean, she's been on loads of these rides before and…"

"Is Millie a trained riding instructor?" I shouted. "If Sally and Jody both think I can do it then that should be fine with Millie, shouldn't it? Just because she's got her own pony and she gets to live here all the time doesn't mean she knows everything, does it?"

Millie glared at me as if she was about to shout back, but then she turned to Gabrielle, saying, "But you can see I'm only saying it because she's my friend, can't you?"

Even Gabrielle got cross then. "I don't know!" she cried. "I only wanted a chocolate digestive, and now you two are putting me in the middle! In fact, I think I'll go and talk to Chloe and Carla and Tam instead!"

And with that she marched off, and me and Millie had a glare at each other and then she marched off too. That was when I spotted Jade looking at me with a smug kind of smile on her face – she'd seen the whole thing. So now Gabrielle is ignoring me and Millie, and us two are ignoring each other. I feel really upset about it and I can't believe that my so-called friends could be so mean. So far they haven't come over here and there's no way I'm going up to either of them. After all, it's their fault we've fallen out, not mine.

I know Jade's still watching me sitting here on my own, so I'm pretending to concentrate really hard on writing this. I don't want her to do that "What are you staring at?" face at me again. I will just have to be Megan the Brave and have a brilliant picnic ride on Mischief and prove everyone wrong – so there!

Thursday, after the ride

It's after tea and we're all watching this film called Spirit in the living room, with yummy hot chocolate and popcorn. I've got the DVD at home and I've seen it about 23 times, so I'm writing this instead. It's quite dark in here so it's hard to keep my writing in a straight line. The film is instead of our Evening Activity, which was meant to be swimming and a barbecue, but it's having a thunderstorm outside so we can't go in the pool. I'm secretly glad because I'm really worn out from the picnic ride and all the terror and excitement that happened to me on it.

So here is the story of…

MEGAN THE BRAVE!

We started our picnic ride with Sally riding at the front and Johnny bringing up the back to make sure we were all safe. It was good

because we had to go down the road a little bit before cutting up on to a lane so we got to use our road safety skills that we did in our lecture this morning, like riding on the verge where we could, keeping together as a group and thanking drivers who come past slowly (well, driver, because there was only one). We all had these bright yellow bibs over our jackets to be visible, too.

I was nervous at first, because after what Jade had said this morning I didn't want one single little thing to go wrong, but it was brilliant riding Mischief out in the countryside and he was really listening to me. But I did feel sad that me and Millie and Gabrielle were still not talking. Millie was at the back, chatting to her dad, and Gabrielle was riding with the younger girls. I didn't feel like I could talk to Kate and Karen as Moody Jade was with them, so I had to ride by myself.

Me on my own

Sally must have noticed because she called for me to trot up to the front of the ride and chat with her. Unlike before when I was too upset to say anything, this time it was a proper chat. She said she was really proud of me for giving it my all with Mischief and she also said how much improvement she could see. I said thanks and how I liked her jacket, because I wanted to say something nice back. We stopped talking after a while and it was good just riding along beside each other. Mischief was a bit keen on some of the trots we did, but I remembered to use my half halts to get him listening and responding to me.

There were some fallen branches and little shrubby things on this grassy bank and Sally let the older girls and Millie and Carla have a go at jumping over them. I even had a pop over a log with Mischief! When Sally said we'd reach the picnic site quite soon, I could hardly believe it. It felt like no time had gone by, but my bottom was getting sore so I could tell it had.

There was a nice gentle uphill-sloping track at the edge of a field of corn and Sally said we could have a canter to the top (everyone can canter now). It was great, flying up the hill with the sound of pounding hooves all around. But then suddenly Mischief was going faster and faster and then he broke into a gallop! As we left the rest of the ride behind us, I panicked and lost my left stirrup. I was desperately trying to get it back and at the same time thinking

◡ Megan and Mischief ◡

For a few seconds I forgot everything I
ever knew about riding. My hands went flying
everywhere and my bottom was bouncing
about and I just clung to Mischief's mane for
dear life. Then finally I caught my breath and
managed to struggle up to sitting. I gathered the
reins, pulled back sharply and shouted, "Whoa!"
but Mischief didn't listen. Trying not to panic,
I focused on getting my stirrup back, hoping
that would give me more control. It took a few
goes but then I got it. I glanced backwards and
everyone else was miles behind.

While I was busy panicking, Mischief veered
off the track and started galloping across the
field instead. Suddenly the hedge into the next
field was looming up ahead of me. It felt a
hundred times scarier than racing up to the
edge of the manège in the gymkhana games
practice and I had no idea how I could make
Mischief stop when he was going so fast!

Well, the answer is that I didn't. He jumped the hedge! Then we were galloping across the next field and I was leaning back and pulling the reins with all my strength and shouting, "Whoa!" as loud as I could, but he still wasn't stopping. Writing it now, it sounds like a long time, but it all went by in a complete flash and I hardly had time to think.

Me and Mischief, very scary!

The hedge I jumped!!

That's when I heard galloping behind me – it was Sally and Millie. Sally kept calling, "Turn him, turn him!" and I tried but nothing happened, and I started to really panic as the next hedge appeared on the horizon. "Megan, turn him NOW!" Sally shouted. "I know you can do it, come on!"

I was just panicking by then and thinking, I can't, I can't! when Millie yelled, "There's a road on the other side of that hedge!"

That really made me listen. I was the rider and I was meant to be in charge, and I couldn't let Mischief get into danger.

"Come on, I know you can do it!" Millie was shouting.

Suddenly I remembered the things Jody had said when we were practising circles and turns. I adjusted my position, took a deep breath and pulled on my right rein, squeezing hard with my left leg. The hedge was really close now and I felt like just shutting my eyes and hoping for the best, but I knew I couldn't give up. I kept my seat and carried on asking Mischief to turn. "Come on, Mischief!" I cried. "We're a team! Just turn for me!" The hedge got closer and closer and then … he turned! It was so sharp I lost my stirrup again, but I didn't care.

"Now circle him!" Sally called. "Quite tight. And use your half halts. That'll slow him down."

Even though it felt like my shoulders were being pulled out of their sockets, I brought him round into a circle. We went round and round and round and it seemed to go on for ever.

Just when I was so scared and tired I felt like leaping off, Mischief dropped into canter and then trot and finally came to a halt. I let the reins go slack with relief and just like that he dropped his head and started eating the grass, as if nothing had happened.

That's when I noticed the rest of the ride standing by the gate – they'd seen everything!

I hardly dared look at Sally – I thought she'd be furious with me! But she just said, "Wow, Megan, that was

AMAZING!"

I must have given her a really confused look because she added, "The way you kept your head and regained control! Just staying on would have been impressive, but you managed to slow him right down, without getting dragged through that hedge!"

"Do you really think he would have jumped it and gone into the road?" I asked.

Sally laughed. "Oh, no, I don't think so. That one's far higher than the last. But saying that, with our Mischief you never can tell. Let's just say, I'm very glad you handled him well and we didn't have to find out!"

Then she said, "Right, let's get back on track. We're not even supposed to be going this way!"

And, signalling for us to follow, she turned and trotted back towards the group by the fence.

Me and Millie looked at each other and both started talking at once. I was saying, "You were

right, I couldn't handle Mischief out here," and Millie was saying, "You were great. You handled him really well. I'm sorry."

Then we steered up close to each other and did the "make friends, make friends" hand-shaking thing to make up, which was quite funny because we had to lean really far over. Sally called out, "Come on, you two, stop horsing around, there's a picnic waiting for us!" and everyone laughed. When we got back to the group, Gabrielle wanted to make up too, so now we're all friends again.

Best friends AGAIN!

80

◡ Megan and Mischief ◡

When Jody arrived in the Land Rover with the picnic, everyone was talking about how brave I was. (I'm not saying that to boast, but it's true, and I did promise to write down everything that happens at Sunnyside!) They kept telling her braver and braver versions of what happened, till it sounded like Mischief had been bucking and rearing and half jumping the hedge and I'd stopped him just by using my little finger.

Then Jade said really loudly to Karen, "She was just showing off, making him gallop like that – it's a miracle she stayed on. She can't even handle him in the manège, let alone out here!"

Everyone turned and looked at me, and Gabrielle started saying, "That's not true!" but I was so annoyed I just stood up for myself without thinking. "Of course I didn't make him do it on purpose!" I shouted. "Unlike you forcing poor Rupert to go near the water. And

at least I stayed on even at a gallop, when you fell off in trot!"

Everyone laughed then, remembering what happened to Jade at the beach. We were staring hard at each other and I was holding my breath, wondering what awful thing she'd say next. But Jade just looked away and I thought, *Wow, I really stood up for myself.* Maybe I can be Megan the Brave with girls too and not just ponies!

★ MEGAN THE BRAVE! ★

When Jody gave me my egg and cress sandwich and Frazzles she winked at me and I winked back – we both knew the secret of how I could turn Mischief and how I could keep him on a circle!

Oh, I'm going to stop writing and watch *Spirit* now because my favourite bit is coming up!

Friday - our last day - boo!

Well, we finally had a midnight feast! Millie told us the headless horseman story and it ended with her going "YOU!" really loudly and making us jump and scream. We had to quickly pretend to be asleep after that because Jody heard the noise and came round with a torch, but then we got up again and ate the strawberry bootlaces and said everything in whispers.

We had to pack up our stuff this morning after breakfast, so we're all ready to go home straight after the gymkhana, because our parents are coming to cheer us on. I'm so excited, and I'm going to try my hardest to win a rosette.

I'm still a bit worried about Jade spoiling things for me, because she hasn't talked to me or even looked at me since I stood up to her.

What if she's planning to do something mean to me at the gymkhana, like running round with her bright pink jacket flapping open to spook Mischief or swapping my egg and spoon race egg for one that's not hard boiled so that it goes all over me?

I'm probably just letting my imagination run away with me – but still, I wish I could know what she's thinking.

Friday afternoon

The gymkhana starts in fifteen minutes, and all
the parents are arriving now. We're meant to
be getting our final things packed, but I did mine
like lightning so I could write in here!

Mischief looks so smart! We had a brilliant
time getting ready for the show after lunch,
with our ponies tied up in the yard so we could
groom them in the sunshine. I didn't even think
a single thought about Jade or what she was
doing or whether she was thinking about me. I
was too busy getting ready for the gymkhana.

Here are all the things I did:

1. First, we all brought our tack out on to
the picnic benches and gave everything a really
good clean and polish.

2. I gave Mischief a really good groom,
including wiping his bottom bits with the special
T sponge (urgh!).

3. I polished his coat with a damp cloth and some conditioning spray until it was really glossy.

4. I combed his mane until it was all smooth and shiny.

5. I tried to plait his tail and weave ribbons into it too, but messed it up, so Lydia showed me how I could just tie some different ribbons round it instead, and that looked really nice.

6. I borrowed some of Millie's hoof oil to make Mischief's hooves really shiny. Gabrielle lent me some sequins as well, but just when I was about to stick them on, Mischief leaned down to my ear and I knew he was trying to tell me he didn't want to look like a girl pony! So I gave the sequins back to Gabrielle and said no thanks after all.

7. I got into my last set of clean riding stuff which I've been saving specially, and Gabrielle did a low ponytail for me with matching ribbons to Mischief's tail.

Even if I don't win any of the races, maybe I will have a chance of winning something in the tack and turnout comp. Mischief certainly deserves it — I think he's the handsomest pony in the world!

STILL Friday afternoon

I am writing this in the car on the way home, because I couldn't wait one single second longer. I'll begin where I left off, so nothing gets missed out.

When we were all ready for the gymkhana we took pictures of each other, so I have loads of photos of me and Mischief to treasure and some great ones of me, Millie and Gabrielle too. Then Jody took some of the whole group together, using each of our phones in turn, so we had to keep smiling for ages and ages. Then—

Oh, I can't tell things in order – I just have to write down the best bits now! Me and Mischief won two rosettes! We got a third place for tack and turnout and also … a first place for the bending race!

○ Megan and Mischief ○

Everything Sally and Jody had taught me about circles and turns really came in useful going round those cones, plus the accidental practice I had on the picnic ride of course! I was neck and neck with Jade and it was really close and before I became Megan the Brave I probably would have let her win to try and make her like me. But not today! I urged Mischief on with my legs and voice, and he seemed to understand my determination and just stepped up the pace a little bit more (without galloping this time, thank goodness). I could hardly believe it when I cantered back over the finishing poles before anyone else.

Millie and Gabrielle and Mum and Dad and Jody and Sally went mad cheering for me. I was so happy I didn't even wonder whether Jade was angry about me winning!

We had loads of fun in the other games too, and I didn't care one bit that Mischief did some

excited bucks in the egg and spoon race and
my egg went flying off to who knows where!

In the Chase Me Charlie I actually got up to
the fourth hole before knocking the pole down.
Sally shouted, "Oh, Megan, you can jump higher
than that!" and everyone who had been on the
picnic ride laughed. I knew she was only joking,
though, and I was really pleased with getting
that far – I'm definitely going to work on my
jumping back at my riding school.

When I went up for winning the bending
race at the prize ceremony, Sally handed me
my rosette and said, "You need speed and
control for that race and you and Mischief
certainly have both now. Well done!"

She shook my hand and
Mum was clapping
like mad and Dad was
snapping away with his
camera.

U Megan and Mischief U

Mum said later that even though her heart was in her mouth (her exact words) watching me do the races she couldn't believe how confident I'd become. I was going to tell her about what happened on the picnic ride but I've decided to wait until she reads this pony diary – she's probably had enough excitement for one day. And she had a present waiting for me in the car too – the army print half chaps! I gave her a big hug of thanks and said, "But how did you know I'd win a race?"

Mum laughed. "They're not for winning, Megan!" she said. "They're for having the courage to go on holiday all on your own."

That's when I realized I was already a bit brave to start off with, to come here without knowing anyone and to make new friends and try new things like beach riding and sandwiches with salady things in.

Maybe Megan the Brave was somewhere inside me all along, but a bit hidden!

I was just heading to the house to get my stuff when Jade came up to me. I thought she might be about to say something mean, but she just held out her hand. Before I could think what I was doing, my hand was shaking hers. "Sorry for being weird with you before," she said. "And well done on winning the bending race."

"It's okay," I mumbled. "And well done in the apple bobbing."

I don't know what changed her mind about me. Maybe she realized I'd stopped caring what she thought, or maybe she just wanted to try on my army print half chaps, but I didn't worry about it. Us girls all said goodbye to each other with lots of hugs, and me and Millie and Gabrielle all swapped e-mail addresses and promised to keep in touch. Then I had to say goodbye to the one person (well, pony!) I would miss most of all, my Mischief.

While the parents all had a cup of tea with Jody and Sally, Lydia and Johnny supervised us on the yard. I led Mischief back to his stable and untacked him, and took out his tail ribbons.

I spent ages untying them so we could have as much time together as possible. While I was making a fuss of him, I whispered in his ear that even if I rode, say, twenty-two more ponies in my life, I would never forget him and he'd always be my favourite. That was when he nuzzled my neck in a way that said, "Even though different kids ride me on Pony Camp each week, you'll always be my favourite too!"

Finally I could hear Dad calling that it was time to go. I gave Mischief one last hug. I felt a bit sad, but mostly I was happy because I had got to meet him in the first place, and because he taught me to be brave. Even though my week at Sunnyside is over, I'll have my memories for ever – and this diary of course!

When I go back to my riding school next week I'm going to carry on being Megan the Brave and ask to go on Dancer or even super-fast Charlie. Well, maybe I'm not ready for him quite yet, but one thing's for sure – no more plodders for me!

PONY CAMP
diaries

Learn all about the world of ponies!

Glossary

Bending – directing the horse to ride correctly around a curve.

Bit – the piece of metal that goes inside the horse's mouth. Part of the bridle.

Chase Me Charlie – a show jumping game where the jumps get higher and higher.

Currycomb – a comb with rows of metal teeth used to clean (to curry) a pony's coat.

Dandy brush – a brush with hard bristles that removes the dirt, hair, and any other debris stirred up by the currycomb.

Frog – the triangular soft part on the underside of the horse's hoof. It's very important to clean around it with a hoof pick.

Girth – the band attached to the saddle and buckled around the horse's barrel to keep the saddle in place.

Grooming – the daily cleaning and caring for the horse to keep it healthy and make it beautiful for competitions. A full groom includes brushing its coat, mane and tail and picking out the hooves.

Gymkhana – a fun event full of races and other competitions.

Hands – a way to measure the height of a horse.

Glossary

Mane – the long hair on the back of a horse's neck. Perfect for plaiting!

Manège – an enclosed training area for horses and their riders.

Numnah – a piece of material that lies under the saddle and stops it from rubbing against the horse's back.

Paces – a horse has four main paces, each made up of an evenly repeated sequence of steps. From slowest to quickest, these are the walk, trot, canter and gallop.

Plodder – a slow, reliable horse.

Pommel – the raised part at the front of the saddle.

Pony – a horse under 14.2 hands in height.

Rosette – a rose-shaped decoration with ribbons awarded as a prize! Usually, a certain colour matches the place you come in during the competition.

Stirrups – foot supports attached to the sides of a horse's saddle.

Tack – the main pieces of the horse's equipment, including the saddle and bridle. Tacking up a horse means getting it ready for riding.

∿ Pony Colours ∾

*Ponies come in all kinds of **colours**. These are some of the most common!*

Bay – Bay ponies have rich brown bodies and black manes, tails and legs.

Black – A true black pony will have no brown hairs and the black can be so pure that it looks a bit blue!

Chestnut – Chestnut ponies have reddish-brown coats that vary from light to dark red with no black points.

Dun – A dun pony has a sandy-coloured body, with a black mane, tail and legs.

Grey – Grey ponies come in a range of colour varieties, including dapple grey, steel grey, and rose grey.

Palomino – Palominos have a sandy-coloured body with a white or cream mane and tail. Their coats can range from pale yellow to bright gold!

Piebald – Piebald ponies have a mixture of black patches and white patches – like a cow!

Skewbald – Skewbald ponies have patches of white and brown.

♋ Pony Markings ♋

*As well as the main body colour, many ponies also have white **markings** on their faces and legs!*

On the legs:

Socks – run up above the fetlock but lower than the knee. The fetlock is the joint above the hoof.

Stockings – extend to at least the bottom of the horse's knee, sometimes higher.

On the face:

Blaze – a wide, straight stripe down the face from in between the eyes to the muzzle.

Snip – a white marking on the horse's muzzle, between the nostrils.

Star – a white marking between the eyes.

Stripe – the same as a blaze but narrower.

White/bald face – a very wide blaze that goes out past the eyes, making most of the horse's face look white!

Fan-tack-stic Cleaning Tips!

*Get your **tack** shining in no time with these top tips!*

- Clean your tack after every use, if you can. Otherwise, make sure you at least rinse the bit under running water and wash off any mud or sweat from your girth after each ride.
- The main things you will need are:
  - bars of saddle soap
  - a soft cloth
  - a sponge
  - a bottle of leather conditioner

- As you clean your bit, check that it has no sharp edges and isn't too worn.
- Use a bridle hook or saddle horse to hold your bridle and saddle as you clean them. If you don't have a saddle horse, you can hang a blanket over a gate. Avoid hanging your bridle on a single hook or nail because the leather might crack!

- Make sure you look carefully at the bridle before undoing it so that you know how to put it back together!
- Use the conditioner to polish the leather of the bridle and saddle and make them sparkle!
- Check under your numnah before you clean it. If the dirt isn't evenly spread on both sides, you might not be sitting evenly as you ride.
- Polish your metalwork occasionally. Cover the leather parts around it with a cloth and only polish the rings – not the mouthpiece, because that would taste horrible!

∾ Grooming Time! ∾

Find out how much you know about caring for your pony with this fun quiz!

1. The first thing to do when grooming is:
   a. Brush your pony's tail.
   b. Apply hoof oil.
   c. Pick out your pony's hooves.

2. The most important reasons to groom your pony are:
   a. To take a break from mucking out, to clean, and to bond.
   b. There's only one – to clean!
   c. To bond, to check for injuries, and to clean.

3. You should groom your pony:
   a. Every week.
   b. Every day.
   c. Every two days.

4. A brush you could use on your pony's face is a:
   a. Body brush.
   b. Metal currycomb.
   c. Plastic currycomb.

5. When grooming, your brush strokes should be:

a. Long and firm.

b. Quick and soft.

c. Slow and cautious.

6. To clean mud off your pony's legs, the best thing to use is a:

a. Cactus cloth.

b. Dandy brush.

c. Body brush.

7. To clean the body brush when grooming your pony:

a. Draw it along a metal currycomb after several strokes, then tap the currycomb on the ground, away from your pony.

b. Rinse it in your pony's water bucket.

c. Wipe it on your jodhpurs after every few strokes.

8. Your pony's mane should never be brushed with a:

a. Mane comb.

b. Body brush.

c. Plastic currycomb.

Answers: 1.c, 2.c, 3.b, 4.a, 5.a, 6.b, 7.a, 8.c

Pretty Plaits!

Follow this step-by-step guide to give your pony a perfect tail plait!

1. Start at the very top of the tail and take two thin bunches of hair from either side, plaiting them into a strand in the centre.

2. Continue to pull in bunches from either side and plait down the centre of the tail.

3. Keep plaiting like this, making sure you're pulling the hair tightly to keep the plait from unravelling!

4. When you reach the end of the dock – where the bone ends – stop taking in bunches from the side but keep plaiting downwards until you run out of hair.

5. Fasten with a plait band!

Gymkhana Ready!

Get your pony looking spectacular for the gymkhana with these grooming ideas!

A running MANE PLAIT

Ribbons on her brow band

Matching ribbons in tail plait

HOOF oil & Sequins on hooves

POLISHED Coat

Turn the page for a sneak peek
at the next story in the series!

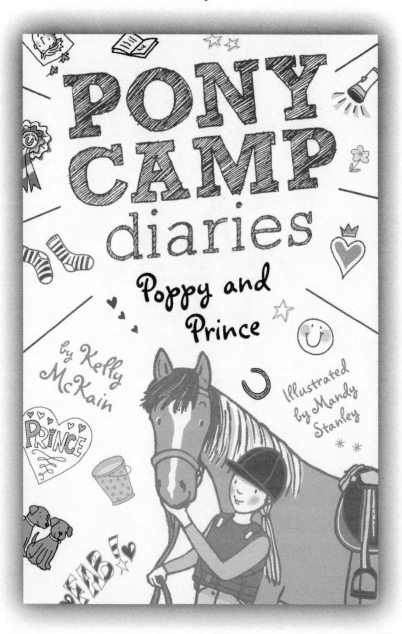

PONY
CAMP
diaries

Poppy and
Prince

by Kelly
McKain

Illustrated
by Mandy
Stanley

PRINCE

FAB!

Monday, at Pony Camp! ☺

Jody's just given me this special diary to write
down all my adventures at Sunnyside Stables.
I'm so glad to be here, it looks like such a great
place – and I'm really excited about riding for
the first time in weeks. On the way in I saw
a field full of lovely ponies and I couldn't help
trying to guess which one will be mine! But I'm
also feeling very nervous because I don't know
if I'll even dare get on her (or him!).

That's because two months ago I had a fall
at my local riding school. They were holding a
show jumping competition and I'd entered the
novice class on my fave pony, Pepper. I went
clear in the first round, and I really wanted to
win, but in round two I got my strides wrong
and jumped the combination a bit long. Pepper
clipped the second set of poles and nearly
fell over – and I came flying off and smacked

right into the wing, then landed strangely on my arm. When I got up, it was hanging at a funny angle – turns out it was broken! It should have really hurt but at the time I couldn't feel anything. Mum said later it was probably because of the shock. When the pain did come on, it was terrible. Two first-aiders made me a sling and helped me out of the manège, and then Mum took me to casualty. I didn't get back on Pepper that day, of course. And my arm took six weeks to heal.

But the fall isn't really the problem (my arm's fine now) – it's what it has done to my confidence. I did try to have a lesson at my stables last week, to get used to things again, but I didn't even manage to get on. I just couldn't make myself do it. It was awful because all the helpers, Hayley (my instructor) and Mum were standing there saying encouraging things,

but I was really dizzy and trembly. In the end I ran off to the loo, pretending I wanted to be sick. And then I stayed in there for ages just feeling so silly and weedy, until Mum banged on the door and took me home.

Right now, I'm sitting on a bench outside the office, which is next to the tack room. There are stables round all three sides of the yard and a gorgeous (and massive) carthorse is peering out at me! It's really cool here because there's a swimming pool (I love swimming) and also these sweet black labs called Viola and Cello, who gave me a big licky cuddle when I arrived! So even if I don't dare to ride this week, I'm sure I can help out on the yard and play  with the dogs and do swimming and stuff – so I'll still have fun. Just hanging around here will be fantastic, and maybe the pony I'm given for the week will help me get back in the saddle again!

I know I shouldn't eavesdrop but I'm
desperately trying to hear what's going on in
the office, because Mum said she would have
a word with Sally and Jody about me losing my
confidence. I feel squirmy with embarrassment
about her telling them, but I'm also relieved
because if they know, they can help me get
back to riding. But – urgh! – I've just had a
horrible thought. What if they say, "Oh yes, yes,
we understand" to Mum, and then when she's
gone they get cross with me if I get scared and
don't want to do things? And what if I can't get
back on and the other girls all laugh?

Oh, it's just so annoying that this has
happened! I wish I could

but I can't.

But maybe it will be easier here because no one knows what I was like before the fall. It's weird to think that I've got a stack of rosettes at home, for show jumping comps and dressage tests and one-day events. Nothing scared me!

But there's no way I'm telling anyone here that, because then they'll expect me to be really good. And just now I'll be happy if I can even sit on a pony!

This lovely girl Lydia has just now asked me if I want to help her pick out Phillip the carthorse's giant feet. If everyone here is as nice as her I should be fine. Right, no more being scared – I've decided that Sunnyside is the perfect place for me to get back in the saddle. I'm going to get on – today!

Still Monday, before the first lesson (gulp!)

My new room-mates have gone down to the yard, but I'm hanging around up here to quickly write what's happened so far.

When everyone came out of the office, Sally spotted me helping out with Phillip and gave me a big smile. "Don't worry, Poppy, we'll get you riding again," she said. So she's nice too – phew! I asked her not to tell anyone else about the fall or about me being so nervous now, and she promised – thank goodness. I don't want anyone feeling sorry for me.

The other girls all started arriving then so I thanked Lydia for letting me do Phillip's feet and followed the crowd upstairs. I'm sharing with this girl Jennifer who has a gingery-brown bob with flicky-up ends. Her suitcase is huge – I think she's brought everything she owns! Our

room is actually Millie's own bedroom (Millie is Jody's daughter) and it's really nice of her to share it with us. Millie has her normal bed by the window and me and Jennifer are in the bunk beds. I said I didn't mind which I had so Jennifer chose the top one. (I was secretly hoping for that one too but making friends is more important!)

They both seem nice, especially Millie, but I think I might have a BIG problem keeping my fall a secret.

When we were unpacking, I kept glancing at Millie and thinking, "I KNOW that girl." And then suddenly I worked out where from. We've both competed in a local show jumping competition – and I beat her! From the second I realized, I was just desperately hoping she wouldn't recognize me, but she soon said, "Haven't I met you before, Poppy?"

I wouldn't usually lie, but I didn't know what to do, and I found myself saying, "Erm, no, I don't think so."

Millie said, "Well, in that case you've got a twin out there who beat me and Tally at the Crewkerne show!"

I made myself grin and reply, "Really? That's

Luckily we got distracted by Jennifer telling us all about her last show jumping competition and re-enacting her fabulous victory. It sounded amazing (almost too amazing to be true, actually). Then she said she could canter a circle on the spot in dressage and Millie instantly cried, "No way! I don't believe that's possible even if you are really, really good unless you're a grown-up professional with a specially trained horse and everything!"

Jennifer looked kind of surprised and embarrassed at the same time. She mumbled, "Well, I haven't actually DONE it yet, but I read about it in *Pony* mag and I reckon I could with a bit of practice."

"Yeah, right!" Millie scoffed. She's so pony-mad she can spot a fib a mile off. Urgh! – I hope she doesn't spot mine!

Jennifer was a bit sniffity after that. She turned

on me and demanded, "What have YOU done, then?" I just completely panicked and blurted out, "Oh, you know, the usual." Then I added, "Hey, I love your fleece," to change the subject.

But Jennifer kept on at me, asking, "But like what, though?"

I went all red and flustered then, like I do in maths when I've been daydreaming and Mr Raines asks me a question. I carried on unpacking and mumbled, "Erm, walk and trot, obviously, some canter and a bit of jumping."

"Oh," she said, "So you're—"

"But only a tiny bit of jumping – pole work mainly," I added quickly, in case she started asking about heights and combinations and all that.

Jennifer just gave me an unimpressed look

and turned back to her bulging suitcase. Phew! I think I got away with it! Of course, I wanted to reveal the truth and shout, "Actually, I am the girl from the Crewkerne show and I've even done cross country and a Pony Club team dressage competition – so there!" But I kept quiet.

Me at the Crewkerne show where I beat Millie and Tally!

Oh, Jody's calling me down to the yard now. Time to meet my pony (hurray!) and see if I dare ride again.

Help!

Still Monday, after lunch - there's just so much to say!

I GOT ON! Thanks to my amazing pony! He's called Prince, and I already love him to bits.

When we'd all gathered on the yard, Jody introduced herself together with Sally and Lydia (she's the nice girl I've already met, and we're supposed to ask her if we need help tacking up and things).

Then all us riders got to meet each other too. There's a beautiful Indian girl called Amita who's about 15, and she's sharing a room with these two friends who've come down from London

together, called April and Amanda – I think
they're both about 13.

Then there's me and Millie and Jennifer......

and lastly some younger girls – Sophie and
Tess and this girl Lucinda who's brought her
own pony with her, a grey Welsh Section A
called Lovely.

Then it was time to meet our ponies! As Lydia led them out there was a lot of squealing and patting and fussing, which made me just feel more and more excited. Then Sally winked at me and said, "We've got the perfect pony for you, Poppy," and out came my gorgeous Prince, a fairly cobby piebald with a really sweet face.

Sally handed me the reins, saying, "Prince is patient and honest, he'll look after you."

I made a big fuss of him, patting him and stroking his muzzle. Then I whispered, "I'm very nervous, Prince. I haven't been on a pony since I had a bad fall. You really *will* look after me, won't you?" Prince pushed his nose against my hand and I just knew that meant yes!

Kelly McKain

Kelly McKain is a best-selling children's and YA author with more than 40 books published in over than 20 languages. She lives in the beautiful Surrey Heath area with her family and loves horses, dancing, yoga, singing, walking and being in nature. She came up with the idea for the Pony Camp Diaries while she was helping young riders at a summer camp, just like the one at Sunnyside Stables! She enjoys hanging out at the Holistic Horse and Pony Centre, where she plays with and rides cute Smartie and practices her natural horsemanship skills with the Quantum Savvy group. Her dream is to do some bareback, bridleless jumping like New Zealand Free Riding ace Alycia Burton, but she has a way to go yet!